CHRISTOPHER ROBIN
LEADS AN EXPEDITION

A. A. MILNE

Christopher Robin Leads an Expedition

Adapted by Stephen Krensky

With decorations by
ERNEST H. SHEPARD

Dutton Children's Books
New York

This presentation copyright © 2003 by the Trustees of the Pooh Properties
From *Winnie-the-Pooh,* copyright © 1926 by E.P. Dutton & Co., Inc.;
copyright renewal 1954 by A. A. Milne.
All rights reserved.

CIP Data is available.

Published in the United States 2003 by Dutton Children's Books,
a division of Penguin Putnam Books for Young Readers
345 Hudson Street, New York, New York 10014
www.penguinputnam.com

Printed in China
First Edition
ISBN 0-525-46824-2
1 3 5 7 9 10 8 6 4 2

CONTENTS

1

IN WHICH CHRISTOPHER ROBIN
REVEALS A PLAN · 7

2

IN WHICH THE EXPEDITION
SETS OUT · 15

3

IN WHICH ROO GOES
FOR A SWIM · 30

4

IN WHICH POOH GETS
SOME RECOGNITION · 38

1

CHRISTOPHER ROBIN REVEALS A PLAN

One fine day

Pooh had stumped up

to the top of the Forest

to see his friend Christopher Robin.

Christopher Robin was sitting outside his

door, putting on his Big Boots.

As soon as he saw the Big Boots,

Pooh knew that an Adventure

was going to happen.

He brushed the honey off his nose

and spruced himself up,

so as to look Ready for Anything.

"Good morning," Pooh called out.

"Hallo, Pooh Bear,"

said Christopher Robin.

"I can't get this boot on.

Do you think you could lean

against me?

I keep pulling so hard

that I fall over backwards."

Pooh sat down,

dug his feet into the ground,

and pushed hard

against Christopher Robin's back.

Christopher Robin pulled and

pulled at his boot until he got it on.

"And that's that," said Pooh.

"What do we do next?"

"We are all going on an Expedition,"

said Christopher Robin.

"Going on an Expotition?"

said Pooh eagerly.

"I don't think I've ever been

on one of those."

"Expedition, silly old Bear,"

explained Christopher Robin.

"It's got an 'x' in it."

"Oh," said Pooh. "I know."

But he didn't really.

"We are going to discover the North Pole,"

said Christopher Robin.

"Oh!" said Pooh again.

"What *is* the North Pole?"

"It's just a thing you discover,"

said Christopher Robin carelessly,

not being quite sure himself.

"Oh! I see," said Pooh.

"Are bears any good at discovering it?"

"Of course they are,"

said Christopher Robin.

"And Rabbit and Kanga

and all of you are going.

That's what an Expedition means.

A long line of everybody.

You'd better tell the others to get ready.

We must all bring Provisions."

"Bring what?" asked Pooh.

"Things to eat."

"Oh!" said Pooh happily.

"I'll go and tell them."

And he stumped off.

2

THE EXPEDITION SETS OUT

The first person Pooh met was Rabbit.

"Hallo, Rabbit," he said.

"I've got a message for you.

We're all going on an Expotition

with Christopher Robin.

And we're all going to discover

a Pole or something."

"We are, are we?" said Rabbit.

"Yes. And we've got to bring

Po—things to eat.

In case we want to eat them.

Now I'm going down to Piglet's.

Tell Kanga, will you?"

Pooh left Rabbit and

hurried down to Piglet's house.

Piglet was sitting on the ground,

blowing happily at a dandelion.

"Oh! Piglet,"

Pooh said excitedly.

"We're going on an Expotition,

all of us.

To discover something."

"To discover what?"

said Piglet anxiously.

"Oh! Just something."

"Nothing fierce?"

"Christopher Robin didn't say

anything about fierce," said Pooh.

"He just said it had an 'x'."

"It isn't their necks I mind,"

said Piglet earnestly.

"It's their teeth.

But if Christopher Robin is coming,

I don't mind anything."

In a little while

they were all ready

at the top of the Forest.

First came

Christopher Robin and Rabbit,

then Piglet and Pooh,

then Kanga, with Roo in her pocket,

and Owl, then Eeyore.

At the end, in a long line, were all

Rabbit's friends-and-relations.

There was a shout

from the top of the line.

"Come on!" called Christopher Robin.

So off they all went to discover the Pole.

As they walked, they chattered to

each other of this and that.

"Hush!" said Christopher Robin.

"We're coming to a Dangerous Place."

They had come to a stream

which twisted and tumbled

between high rocky banks.

"It's just the place for an Ambush,"

Christopher Robin explained.

"What sort of bush?"

whispered Pooh to Piglet.

"A gorse-bush?"

"My dear Pooh," said Owl,

"don't you know what an Ambush is?

It's a sort of Surprise."

"So is a gorse-bush sometimes,"

said Pooh.

"If people jump out at you suddenly,

that's an Ambush," said Owl.

Pooh said that a gorse-bush

had sprung at him suddenly one day

when he fell out of a tree.

They were climbing up the stream now,

going from rock to rock.

After they had gone a little way,

they came to a place where the banks

widened out to a level strip of grass.

"Halt!" called Christopher Robin.

"I think we ought to eat

all our Provisions now,

so that we won't have so much to carry.

Have you all got something?"

"All except me," said Eeyore.

"As Usual."

He looked round at them.

"I suppose none of you are sitting

on a thistle by any chance?"

"I believe I am," said Pooh. "Ow!"

He got up and looked behind him.

"Yes, I was. I thought so."

"Thank you, Pooh," said Eeyore.

"If you've quite finished with it."

He moved across to Pooh's place

and began to eat.

As soon as he had finished his lunch,

Christopher Robin whispered to Rabbit,

and they walked a little way

up the stream together.

"I didn't want the others to hear,"

said Christopher Robin.

"Quite so," said Rabbit.

"It's—I wondered—It's only—"

began Christopher Robin.

"Rabbit, what does the North Pole

look like?

I did know once,

only I've sort of forgotten."

"It's a funny thing," said Rabbit,

"but I've forgotten, too."

"I suppose it's just a pole stuck in

the ground," said Christopher Robin.

"And if it's a pole," said Rabbit,

"it would be sticking in the

ground, because there'd be

nowhere else to stick it.

The only thing is,

where is it sticking?"

3

ROO GOES
FOR A SWIM

They went back to the others.

Piglet was lying on his back,

sleeping peacefully.

Roo was washing his face

and paws in the stream.

Kanga proudly explained that this

was the first time Roo had ever

washed his face himself.

"I don't hold with all

this washing," said Eeyore.

"What do *you* think, Pooh?"

"Well," said Pooh, "*I* think—"

There came a sudden

squeak from Roo,

a splash, and a loud cry

of alarm from Kanga.

"Roo's fallen in!" cried Rabbit.

He and Christopher Robin came

rushing down to the rescue.

"Look at me swimming!" squeaked Roo

from the middle of the pool.

"Are you all right, Roo dear?"

called Kanga anxiously.

"Yes!" said Roo. "Look at me sw—"

and down he went over a waterfall

into another pool.

Everyone was doing something to help.

Piglet was jumping up and down

and making "Oo, I say" noises.

Owl was explaining that

the Important Thing was

to Keep the Head Above Water.

Eeyore had turned round

and hung his tail over the first pool.

"Catch on to my tail, little Roo,"

he said, "and you'll be all right."

"Get something across the stream

lower down," called Rabbit.

But Pooh was already

getting something.

Two pools below Roo

he was standing with a long pole

in his paws.

Kanga came up, and between them

they held it across the

lower part of the pool.

Roo drifted up against it

and climbed out.

"Pooh, did you see me swimming?"

squeaked Roo.

"That's called swimming,

what I was doing.

Rabbit, did you see

what I was doing?"

"Swimming.

Hallo, Piglet!

What do you think I was doing!

Swimming!

Christopher Robin,

did you see me—"

But Christopher Robin

wasn't listening.

He was looking at Pooh.

4

POOH GETS
SOME RECOGNITION

"Pooh," said Christopher Robin,

"where did you find that pole?"

Pooh looked at the pole in his hands.

"I just found it," he said.

"I thought it ought to be useful."

"Pooh," said Christopher Robin
solemnly, "the Expedition is over.
You have found the North Pole!"

"Oh!" said Pooh.

Eeyore was sitting with his tail in the

water when they all got back to him.

"Here I am!" squeaked Roo.

Eeyore took his tail

out of the water

and swished it from side to side.

"As I expected," he said.

"Lost all feeling. Numbed it."

"Poor old Eeyore.

I'll dry it for you,"

said Christopher Robin,

taking out his handkerchief.

"Thank you," said Eeyore.

"You're the only one who seems

to understand about tails.

A tail isn't a tail to *them,*

it's just a Little Bit Extra at the back."

"Hullo, Eeyore," said Pooh,

coming up to them with his pole.

"Hullo, Pooh. Thank you for asking.

I shall be able to use it again

in a day or two."

"Use what?" asked Pooh.

"What are we talking about?"

asked Eeyore.

"I wasn't talking about anything,"

said Pooh, looking puzzled.

"My mistake again.

I thought you were saying

how sorry you were about

my tail being all numb,

and could you do anything to help?"

"No," said Pooh, "that wasn't me."

He thought for a little.

"Perhaps it was somebody else,"

he suggested helpfully.

"Well, thank him for me

when you see him."

Pooh looked anxiously at Christopher Robin.

"Pooh's found the North Pole,"

said Christopher Robin.

"Isn't that lovely?"

Pooh looked modestly down.

They stuck the pole

in the ground,

and Christopher Robin tied

a message on to it.

NORTH POLE

DISCOVERED BY POOH

POOH FOUND IT.

Then they all went home again.

Roo had a hot bath

and went straight to bed.

But Pooh went back to his own house,

and feeling very proud

of what he had done,

had a little something

to revive himself.